This book belongs to …

....

Tips for Talking and Reading Together

Stories are an enjoyable and reassuring way of introducing children to new experiences.

Before you read the story:

● Talk about the title and the picture on the cover. Ask your child what they think the story might be about.

● Talk about what recycling is. Show your child the recycling bins you have at home or in your local area.

Read the story with your child. After you have read the story:

● Discuss the Talk About ideas on page 27.

● Talk about the things that we can recycle on pages 28-29. Do the activity, and see which things you can find in the pictures of the story.

● Do the fun activity on page 30.

Have fun!

Find the 10 pink shells hidden in the pictures.

For more hints and tips on helping your child become a successful and enthusiastic reader look at our website www.oxfordowl.co.uk.

Let's Recycle!

Written by Roderick Hunt
and Annemarie Young
Illustrated by Alex Brychta

OXFORD
UNIVERSITY PRESS

The family was camping at the seaside. Dad was painting something.

"What are you doing?" asked Mum.

"I'm painting this empty snail shell purple," said Dad.
"It's for a game to play on the beach."

5

Later on, Wilf and Wilma arrived with their parents.
"We saved the spot next to us for your tent," said Dad.

"Thanks," said Wilma's dad. The family started unpacking and began to settle in.

"This will be fun," said Kipper.

"I'll cook a barbecue for us all," said Wilma's dad.

"Thanks," said Mum. "We can go and explore the beach."

"I'll get rid of this rubbish," said Dad. "They have good recycling bins here. There's even one for food waste."

The beach was in a sandy cove.

There were rocks to climb, rock pools to look in and a cave to explore.

While the children were paddling in the sea, Dad hid his purple snail shell among the rocks.

"Sometimes, a rare shell can be found here," said Dad.
"It's the purple sea snail. It's really lucky to find it."

"I'll give a prize to anyone who finds one," he said. The children raced off to search for a purple shell.

Wilf, Biff and Kipper searched along the shore line.

"Ugh!" said Kipper. "Look at all these plastic bottles."

Chip and Wilma searched among the rocks and rock pools.

"All this litter!" said Chip. "I can see two plastic bags in this pool."

Suddenly, something moved behind a rock. A seagull was tangled in the plastic rings from some drink cans, so it couldn't fly.

Dad held the gull carefully in his sweater and Mum untangled it. The gull hopped and then flew away.

"Why do people leave litter on beaches?" said Wilma.
"Look at the harm it can do to wildlife!"

The children collected as much litter as they could.
Wilma's mum got something to put it in.

"We're learning about recycling at school," said Biff. "Cans can be recycled, and paper can be recycled up to six times!"

"Do you know that duvet filling can be made from recycled plastic bottles?" said Wilf. "So we could be sleeping under plastic bottles!"

"Well," said Dad. "The beach is much cleaner now, thanks to you. Let's wash our hands, then see who can find a purple sea snail!"

"There are bits of broken purple shell by this rock," said Mum.

Oh no! Someone had trodden on Dad's shell by mistake.

When they got back, Wilf's dad had made a delicious barbecue.

"There won't be much leftover food to recycle," said Wilf.

"Sleep well," said Dad. "It's been a busy day."

"We never did find the purple sea snail," said Chip, with a yawn.

Mum went to bed but Dad stayed outside. He had a little job to do.

"Bedtime," Mum called, softly. "I won't be long," whispered Dad.

Talk about the story

Why did Dad paint a snail shell?

What did the children do with the litter they found on the beach?

How did Wilma feel when they found the seagull?

What do you recycle at home?

Sort the rubbish

Which recycling bins would you put these things into?

Which of these things can you find in the pictures of the story?

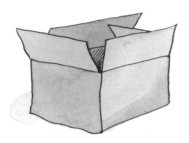  

Glass

Cardboard

Cans

Food Waste

Plastic

Paper

Snail trail maze

Help Kipper find the purple sea snail.

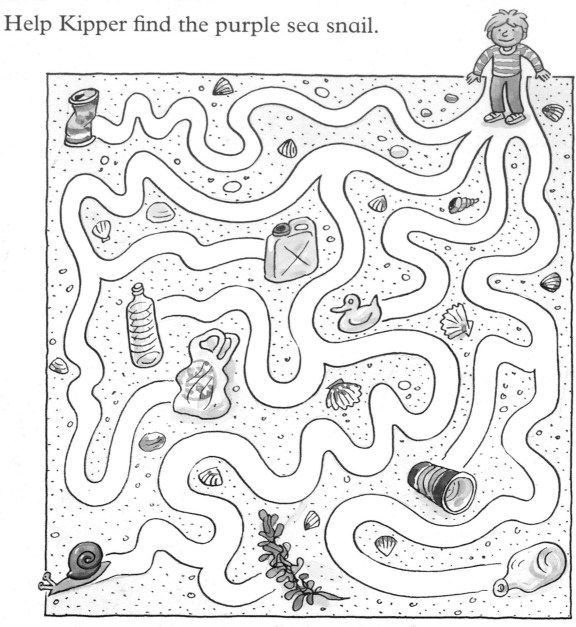

FIRST EXPERIENCES WITH Biff, Chip & Kipper

Have you read them all yet?

Kipper's First Pet

Learning to Swim

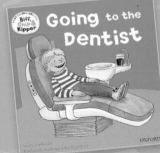

Going to the Dentist

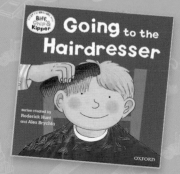

Going to the Hairdresser

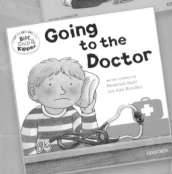

Going to the Doctor

Going on a Plane

Let's Recycle!

Fun at the Farm

Starting School

Kipper Gets Nits

Going on a Train

FIRST EXPERIENCES Flashcards
55 cards

Also available:
- **At the Hospital**
- **At the Optician**
- **At the Vet**
- **At the Match**
- **At the Dance Class**

Read with Biff, Chip and Kipper
The UK's best-selling home reading series

Phonics

First Stories

	Phonics				First Stories			
Level 1 Getting ready to read	Kipper's Alphabet I Spy	Chip's Letter Sounds	Biff's Wonder Words	Floppy's Fun Phonics	Get On	Floppy Did This!	Up You Go	Six in a Bed
Level 2 Starting to read	I am Kipper	Cat in a Bag	The Red Hen	The Fizz-Buzz	Funny Fish	Silly Races!	The Snowman	Dad's Birthday
Level 3 Becoming a reader	Such a Fuss	Shops	The Sing Song	The Backpack	Poor Old Rabbit	I Can Trick a Tiger	Super Dad	Floppy and the Bone
Level 4 Developing as a reader	Wet Feet	The Moon Jet	The Red Coat	Quick! Quick!	Missing!	The Raft Race	Dragon Danger	The Spaceship
Level 5 Building confidence in reading	Egg Fried Rice	Craig Saves the Day	Seasick	Dolphin Rescue	Hungry Floppy	Husky Adventure	Trapped!	Looking after Gran
Level 6 Reading with confidence	Gran's New Blue Shoes	Ice City	Save Pudding Wood	Uncle Max	Hairy-Scary Monster	Mountain Rescue	The Lost Voice	Secret of the Sands

Phonics stories help children practise their sounds and letters, as they learn to do in school.

First Stories have been specially written to provide practice in reading everyday language.

OXFORD
UNIVERSITY PRESS

Great Clarendon Street, Oxford OX2 6DP
Text © Roderick Hunt and Annemarie Young 2009
Illustrations © Alex Brychta 2009
First published 2009
This edition published 2012

10 9 8 7 6 5 4 3 2 1
Series Editors: Kate Ruttle, Annemarie Young
British Library Cataloguing in Publication Data available
ISBN: 978-0-19-273512-6
Printed in China by Imago
The characters in this work are the original creation of Roderick Hunt and Alex Brychta who retain copyright in the characters.
With thanks to Suzanne Eden and John Hunt